for mark

VIKING
Published by the Penguin Group
Penguin Putnam Books for Young Readers, 345 Hudson Street,
New York, New York 10014, U.S.A.
Penguin Books Ltd, 27 Wrights Lane, London W8 5TZ, England
Penguin Books Australia Ltd, Ringwood, Victoria, Australia
Penguin Books Canada Ltd, 10 Alcorn Avenue, Toronto, Ontario, Canada M4V 3B2
Penguin Books (N.Z.) Ltd, 182-190 Wairau Road, Auckland 10, New Zealand
Penguin Books Ltd, Registered Offices: Harmondsworth, Middlesex, England
First published in 2001 by Viking, a division of Penguin Putnam Books for Young Readers.

1 2 3 4 5 6 7 8 9 10

Printed in Mexico
Set in Swiss721 Bold Round
Book design by Megan Montague Cash and Angela Carlino

LIBRARY OF CONGRESS CATALOGING-IN-PUBLICATION DATA
Cash, Megan Montague.
I saw the sea and the sea saw me / by Megan Montague Cash.
p. cm.
Summary: A girl enjoys using all of her five senses to explore the ocean, but when a
jellyfish appears she discovers that the sea is not always nice.
ISBN 0-670-89966-6 (hardcover)
[1. Beaches—Fiction. 2. Jellyfishes—Fiction. 3. Stories in rhyme.]
I. Title.
PZ8.3.C272 Iae 2001
[E]—dc21
00-011939

I Saw
the Sea
and
the Sea
Saw Me

megan montague cash

viking

I saw the sea
and the sea saw me.

I saw the stripe of bluish blue.

My bathing suit had blue stripes too.

I heard the sea

and the sea heard me.

The sound I heard was miles tall.

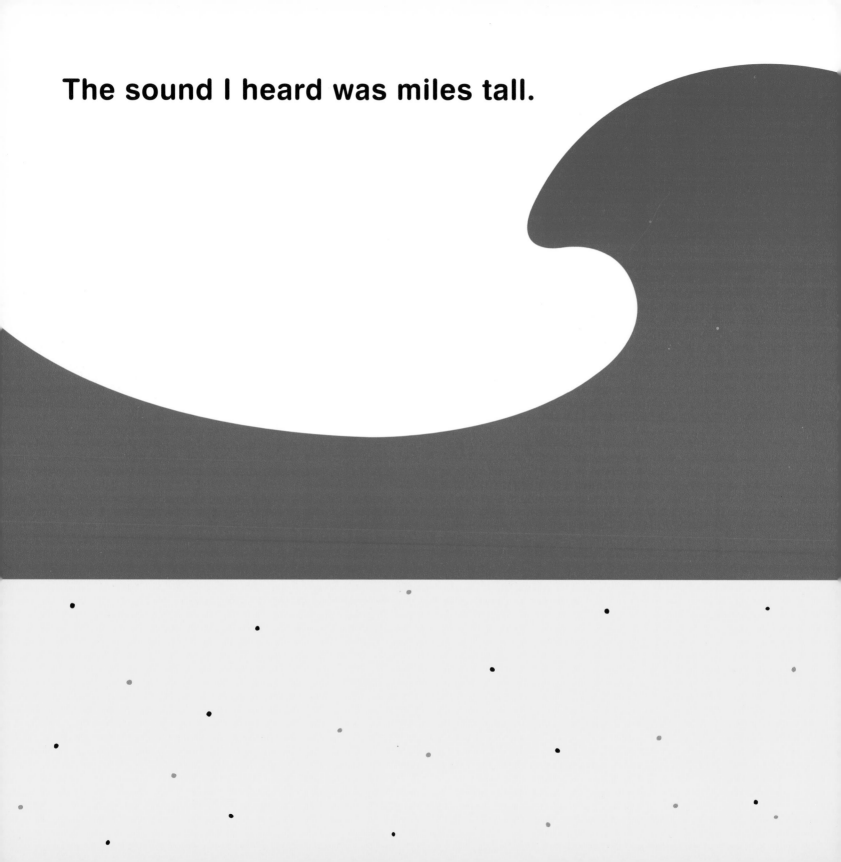

My biggest sound seemed very small.

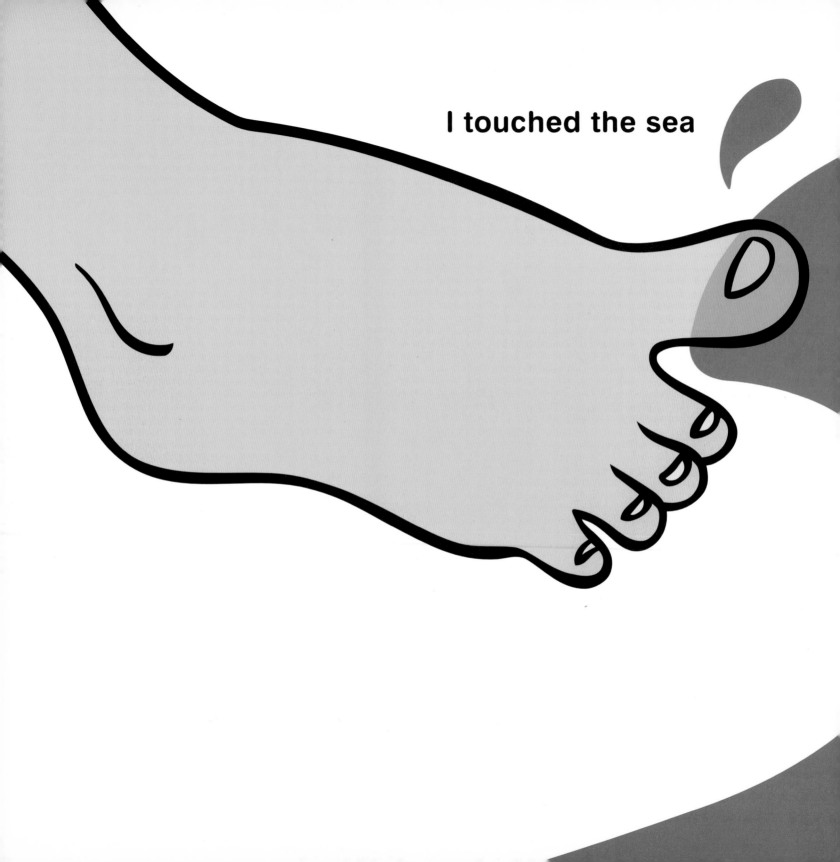

I touched the sea

and the sea touched me.

I touched the cold and foamy wet.

We splashed and danced each time we met.

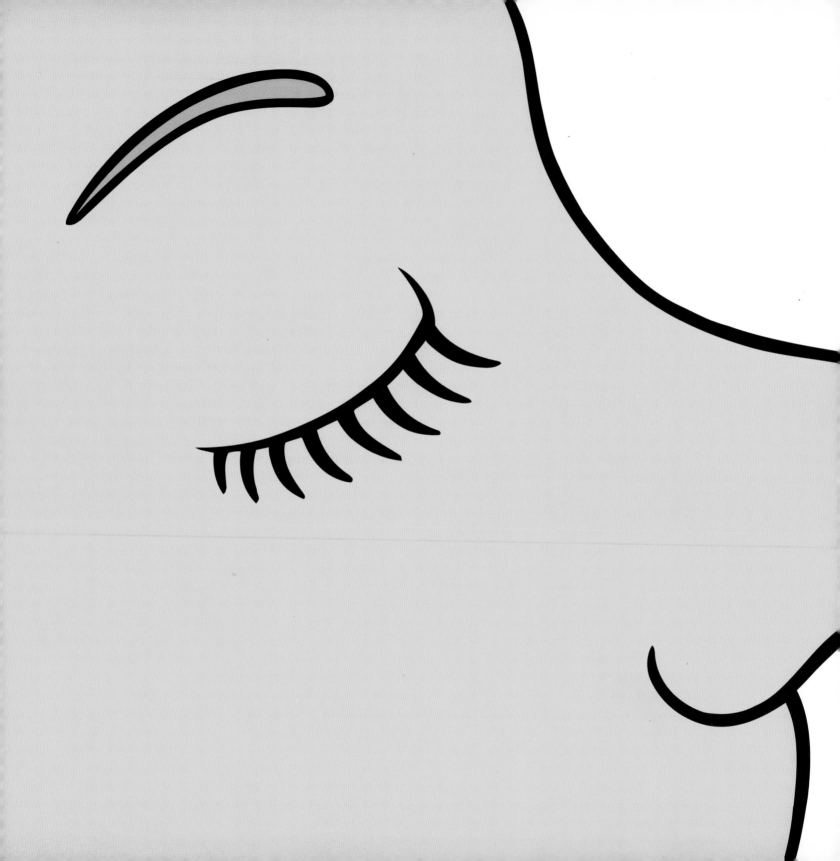

I smelled the sea

and the sea smelled me.

The salty smell was in the air,
with seaweed tangled in my hair.

I tasted the sea

and the sea tasted me.

I tasted more salt on my tongue.

I'd be there now, but I got . . .

Stupid water!

Stupid land!

Stupid salt!

And stupid sand!

Take me home!

Now I wash my seaweed hair.

I'm in the bathtub. I don't care.

Tonight I'll dream about the sea.

I wonder if she dreams of me?